Miles Traveled Down Love's Highway

Kefentse Booth

ISBN 978-0-9977409-0-5
eBook ISBN 978-0-9977409-1-2

Published by Street Light Dreams, LLC, Detroit, MI
www.StreetLightDreams.com

This book is dedicated to May Y. Booth.

It's not a day that goes by that I don't search for your warmth.

Table of Contents

Introduction

I was young when the pen graced my hands. My mother was an English teacher in the Detroit Public Schools System, yet I was the kid that didn't follow the rules often. My mother made me read literature, in addition to my daily school work, as a form of punishment. Unbeknownst to her, that pen and notebook were the only things that listened to me without judgment.

My imagination pierced the pages every time I sat down to write. Hour after hour, I sat in my own world, recreating the scenery my eyes had once witnessed. Coming from where I'm from, you saw more imagery than in the movies. I often took the lives of my peers and candidly exaggerated their plights to protect their identity.

This book serves as a comprehensive storyboard for women through a man's eyes. With poetic storytelling that could paint a million pictures per piece into the reader's mind, one will be intertwined into a creative imagery of daily outtakes within a relationship. Through situational experiences, the short stories became independent stories, but without any outlined characters. I wouldn't dare pigeonhole the reader with false identification of a functional character when life throws so many situations into our lives that are relatable.

Each passage offers the reader vivid pictures, which lead into thought-provoking dialogue. *Miles Traveled Down Love's*

Highway is written in two parts. The first part lays the foundation of the journey it takes to commit and fall in love unconditionally.

Though published several times for custom essays, the thought of putting these works into a full book seemed daunting. I scribbled in notebooks during class while I was in school, pulling the paper out of the notebook and leaving it lying around the house. My mother placed my notes in a binder, but not before she proofread and corrected my spelling and grammatical errors. One day, she presented them to me and encouraged me to publish the work. She'd compiled pieces from as early as third grade, when I'd just learned to write cursive, all the way into my college years.

I finally compiled this book, and the smile on my mother's face just scratched the surface of her admiration for my literature. She, maybe even more than I, dreamed of my work touching the masses through my words.

My mother lay on a hospital bed, waiting on a doctor to diagnose the pain in her shoulder. Passing the time, she read through this book you hold today. She blessed the content minutes prior to being diagnosed with a treatable cancer in April of 2015. One minute, I was making my mother proud. The next minute, I was consoling her greatest fear, trying not to cry from the inside out.

My greatest fan, my mentor of my talents, passed away in September of 2015. Five months after seeing her smile with excitement, I found myself staring at the same pen and pad she placed in my life, motionless. Never did I imagine that her name would appear in the dedication stating, "In Loving

Memory," instead of giving her thanks and glory for all she sowed into me. Here you hold my most intimate work, along with the dream of mother and child.

Preface

I kicked so many stones down the highway of life. Alone and afraid to grow, I trekked down paths, finding exits on my highway.

It was the way love entered my life that made me feel like I was speeding down love's highway. Steep hills with curves, being cornered at uncontrollable speeds, I was looking for an exit. Miles quickly accumulating, the relationships traveled, too, were named after cities in my eyes.

The wear and tear affected my heart. I was stagnant on my journey through life, the leisure of going as I pleased becoming a weight. I battled looking for that special someone, playing the field of endless possibilities that left small parts of my soul strewn on the road at every stop.

I reminisce on the touch they had on my body. Their willingness to accept my limits, never requiring my full commitment. While many asked for my heart and time, my unsuccessful attempts always ended with tears and hurtful words.

Love's highway carried me on a rollercoaster ride of emotions and misunderstanding. It was the pavement on which my vehicle traveled down, yet never reaching the intended destination.

I drove north and south, explored east and west. Yet, still my heart stayed with me. I found the willing, but never located the completion. Many close calls impaired my thought process, with family still giving me the side eye for ignoring the warning signs.

Then it happened. I coerced myself into giving my all, letting go of my tainted past. Maybe it wasn't them. Maybe it was me. Maybe I didn't have the wherewithal to mature a relationship into something greater. After a spiritual system flush and proper burial of skeletons, we collided at an intersection. Catching eyes and conversing, our characteristics flirted with each other. I accepted the heart of this beautiful woman, accepting her confession of love. Together, we journeyed down the highway many have come to know as *love*.

Miles Traveled in Love

I can't explain the miles I've traveled with you. I can't fathom words that could express the gratitude that I have for your beautiful spirit. How does one repay a debt with immeasurable cost? I reflect on the love of connection, the understanding of our misunderstood characteristics. I never saw the world from a viewpoint of heightened aura, like yours. I never saw the calm of a wind pass me by and deliver chills that caused a smile of uplifting nature.

The Lord molded a phenomenal woman when He breathed life into your lungs. You find a way to release the life you cherish into the warm-blooded hearts of the protectors you encounter along life's highway. I walked the same distance, but traveled light years in your company. Your picture reeled in my wants and talents, and blew mesmerizing dust in my face to achieve the talents the Lord deposited into me.

How do I repay a person with no communication? How do I give to an entity that may never receive the present? Time evolves and life carries on, yet days at a time, I reflect on your friendship. Days on end, I peek into your thoughts, but I can't feel the beat of your heart. I love deeper because of you. I love to the depths 'cause you showed me that time doesn't lend timing to situations like we plan. I lost a touch that I never physically touched. I lost a beat of a heart that had power in its rhythm and blues. I never smelled your custom scent. I never breathed your air. I never used my fingerprints to imprint my touch into caressing your wants into reality. I never used the many nerves of my lips to kiss the pain away from your life.

Yet, in my blinded vision, within an array of colors, I see you. I see your drive for me. I see your prayers for my wellbeing. I pen a thought with your wisdom in the wording. I plagiarize a space in life where the connection of two felt like one. I engulf my soul into a transversal that connects the fibers of existence. I hold on to more than you might be holding, probably because I never told you the thoughts I wished I surrendered to your ears. I look deep into a computer screen, deep into your eyes through an Internet photo. That's when I realize that we let go so we could go farther than we should know. We let go in order to be all that we had stored within our talents present by the Lord. So, to the friend who touched my life during a time I was moving into a realm of excellence, I thank you for *you*. Although we never talk, we talked the future into the presence of today's endeavors. Continue to be more than the understanding of life. Stay grounded to the words that coat the heart and soul of an obedient vessel. You taught a blind me how to cross the street in moving traffic with no touch from a guiding hand. You showed me that friendship comes without asking, but lasts through disconnect. The morals of life are embedded in the atoms of its creation.

With This Love of Ours

With this love of ours, I'm past the initial love. I'm head over heels into a realm that has me scared to depart. We break away from one another daily, and my heart reaches for more. My arms grab, hug and pull her closer, tugging on the affection of her blissful love. The soft tissues of her lips make the goodnight kisses irresistible to disconnect. This is a new story with a body of work that the most talented writer couldn't inscribe.

Quite simply, she fits. The feeling of connection has me wondering if she carries my rib. I'm mesmerized in so many ways that I don't even think about the days on the calendar as they change. We talk like kids, endless speaking engagements with one another as the attentive audience. I'm adorned by a smile that only she could engrave on my face. She thinks outside the box, infusing the two different worlds we reside in into one stratosphere. Yet, for me, I gave so much to this world that I plan on giving her the universe. Maybe I'll gift a distant nebular with new constellations for us to name, or build permanent property on "Cloud 9" and charge a small entrance fee into the state of our love.

We are at the selfish junction of relationship wants. We are holding on 'til our eyes get heavy. Personally, I don't plan on leaving unless the Lord pulls me off assignment. Until that day never happens, I will protect, honor, love, cherish and grow with her. I shall push her to be nothing less than the excellence that makes up the blood in her veins. Allow her muscles to stay fit on the push-ups of the new status bar she lifts higher daily. I stare into her eyes and I see an unbelievable moment. I stare longer and see a believable future. Whatever she sees in me will never leave. I just pray the evolution of me doesn't hinder the evolution of us. In God I trust, in Him I confide. For He knows the things I search for, yet He blessed me with an angel to walk by my side.

Fallen

I love her. It's odd to say, but my heart knows this to be true. I walked through life holding on to so much "me" that I never cared about "us" first. Yet, she's different. Something about her eases my soul, like prayers during the witching hour. I search for confirmation, but everything leads me down a road that exceeds anything that's ever done for others. She is different and her presence is all over me.

I am shouting, "Love!" as I climb mountains. I want all to hear my cry of joy. She stares at me, her eyes showing admiration as to why I came. I'm here now. Nothing but us can stop this connection. She studies me and likewise, I study her. My prayers do have an answer and I call them by her name. Heightened spirituality is where we rest our fate. We pray heavenly for direction, knowing the Lord directed our mingling minds. I asked for some things and compromising isn't in the equation. We derived a hypothesis mathematically, challenging those that don't believe in our Savior.

She is my "B," me being her "A." Together, we work for the completion of "C." The equal sign rests between us. It spaces our present on the left side and equates the future on the right. I stare at pure love; rare in form, but unconditional in essence. The difference in her is outlined in a language that can only be translated by the Lord. I prayed for an angel. I said I'd give up everything for a feel of what I write. I prayed to the Lord for her, even when my soul barely recognized the

Lord's voice. But I heard Him vaguely and moved closer to His presence.

She stayed at the forefront of my needs, but the Lord strengthened me first. What He presented to me couldn't be wrapped in my darkened, old state. Anew He made me, gifting me with a blank canvas to paint a portrait with her. She releases bits of her soul daily as we form structure in the Lord's eyes. I love her because time is of the essence and she makes her essence the time of my life. I love her because she is me, the completion of my life-long puzzle. Who knew she'd hold the missing pieces? I love her because she loves the Lord, showing me that guided steps of sacrifice do pay a dividend of heavenly riches.

Hourglass Eyes

Her eyes have me seeing things. They have me spellbound and navigating deep into the stories they tell. The soft brown pupils are projection reels with panoramic viewpoints of her life. Arched eyebrows illuminate her gorgeousness as the rainbow-shaped art complements the two tear drop optics. I'm motionless by beauty when I stare deeply. She allows me entry through the emotions those eyes yell. I listen to the frustration, the loving desires of a future connection with the heart and soul that the Lord has formed for her.

Those hourglass eyes show a lifetime eclipsed. Yet the passion and drive they also carry give off her faith and confidence. I burrow into her soul for clarity. She allows me in and I look out the sands of her eyes--speckles of her past, the smiles and heartburn that cause redness to form tears. I hear the voice of this angel that wants love, the voice of an angel that wants a touch of Heaven while she lives out her days on Earth.

Those hourglass eyes are more than her sight that guides her around this world. They are the focal point of her showing me everything needed to exist in her aura, a one-off tutorial that gives the answers to her test of life once administrated. The beauty of those eyes pours out, sings the lullabies of love, and suspends a life prior to grace her with a new one. I'm compelled with fascination and she is engulfed in inspiration. I'm honored to count each grain of sand to the very end, enjoying companionship on the journey, while looking deeply into her hourglass eyes.

Made To Love

I fell in love with something I never want to leave, something that allows me to fall in love without any boundaries boxing me in. I traveled down paths in this life that I never knew the direction, but they all lead to you. I went searching for answers without ever asking the question. You showed up with the posse of a queen in demand of a king.

We grew together, leaps and bounds to figure out a language of love that only skilled lovers could dissect. We complement one another in our individual endeavors, yet we dream dreams together of an inseparable future. How does one comprehend the evolution of time? Must be just as mind blowing as true love and the measures one takes to never lose it.

As for me, I'll go to the Earth's end and fall off the map into a new world to prove my love. I'll take a spaceship and present you with a distant star to light up your night. Let it twinkle in a room where we pray to the heavens for obedience and guidance. Make a wish on that star to give a fairytale smile to an angelic face I have fallen in love with.

Life pulled a fast one on me. Never did I expect the life I have lived to be so complete in the last couple of years. Never did I think that love was able to teach as well show my future all in the same instance.

I try so hard to never lose my grip on love. I try to never get complacent with showing you that it's only you--the rest of the world are onlookers into a theatrical play that the Lord has written for all to see. All can have this same masterpiece if only they trust in the power of the love He provides.

I present you with my heart. Please open it and find refuge there. You will be safe as I protect you from the adversity of this world. Let me provide and create a life that is funneled directly from Heaven. Believe in me, as I believe in my faith.

I gave it all to Him for blessings and endless time. Let me give it all to you for appeasing tears and the fulfillment of more. I will forever look into your eyes for admiration and trust. Rest in my heart for a connection with a man who wants to be more than the life he lives for himself. I want to be all the life for you and the family that the future has granted for us.

Rest assured that the blood in my heart pumps the same beat as the one that's nestled in your chest cavity. But, most of all, our souls connect to a Heaven with one Lord that we give it all to for this relationship to be a worthy servant of His mighty power.

Savory Taste of Love

It's the language we speak that has my mind mentally stimulated. The dissertation within our conversations yields transforming revelations. It's the hue of the caramel skin that invites the sweet taste that I indulge in. Aromatherapy takes my breath away as my pallets savor over you. It's something about each nerve on those lovely lips that leaves me kissing for hours. Maybe it's the small of your back and how you soak into my arms. The massage I administer deflates the tensions of life away with my grip.

Could it be the resting place you warrant as a pillow as you nestle your head deeply into the indention of my chest? For every loose string of hair that sits atop of your head, I count the endless ways I love to love you. We stand so strong together. But on bended knee, I rest as you answer. In front of a body of our peers, we vow to the Lord as the angels serenade us in the winds.

Forever my friend, my heart's desires propel into prayers for achievement. You are the gift from God I asked for when I saw no face to love. You are that figure in my eyesight that leaves teeth prints on my lower lip.

You're more than the physical attributes that bless your existence. You're more than the sight of a driven woman with the pulse on greatness. You are the one I want to share every breath with, sharing air that can't be seen into our lungs for completion. You are the beginning of my day and the end of my night. You are the understanding of dreams that have realistic touch. You are the hold on my heart that warms it to never be cold and detached. You are the love I write about and the ink that bleeds the passion for words. You are the muse I envision when my sight has failed me. You are the future to my current stronghold.

I will rub the womb that is pleased to bear the children we create. I will rub the follicles of your hair and stroke your mental worries aside from that angelic face of yours. I will blanket the transgressions of tomorrow with our prayers of today. I'll give you a dollar for every compliment I give you and witness the riches through your smiles and blushing cheeks.

You're the rib that fits into my lonely socket, looking for its mate. You're the last of a dying breed that resuscitated me with working lungs. You would give me your breath to pump a part of your love. You held my body as it warmed from your majestic touch. I cried to the heavens for you in my life--you were sent to save me. For that, I present all of my future and nothing of my past. I give you my all and nothing less. I give you the life authors write about in love stories and casually walk with you through every chapter as we build together. You are the most precious gift ever given to me-the most precious piece to a puzzle that needed you for maximum completion. You are the future of my today and the starting point of my forever. This is the introduction to "A Real Love Story." I humbly sign it as your helpmate.

Where Love Can Take You

If words could talk, you would read this silently and they would boast a loud roar.

My point would get across, as if it were a plane. The message would pass the constellations as it soars.

The nebular hypothesis of our love would give a dissertation worthy of a doctorate in Philosophy.

The hands you hold the page with would grip the fibers of the body of thoughts; your mind would be fabricated.

Your fingers would be injected with my scriblical insight; my love would be insinuated.

The cornea would focus. Your eardrum would hear the voice on the page.

The adrenaline will rush through your veins, but in the most seductive rage.

As your visions move from line to line, your heart rapidly beats as the words engulf you in time.

The essence of life floats you away to heavenly heights imagined by romantics.

Your feet lift off the floor, and you're now hugging the paper for my soul's protection.

Knees weaken as the acceptance of love flows toward your feet.

Whatever you were doing before you started reading now becomes obsolete and bleak.

The ink from my words bleeds onto your shirt as the tears hit the canvas that houses my feelings.

It is written to take my hand; you release your grip because you are ready and willing.

The room is empty to sight, yet the connection of souls has its presence light years away.

Through the canvas, my hand reaches out--never once will I lead you astray.

Never once would I play with your mind, body and soul.

I will never leave you emotionally alone, closing the door and leaving you in the cold.

The crosswise of our hearts unite as the vision is generated through eyesight.

The cloudy dust in the universe forms a new planet. We land on it with our passion as we follow the light.

I finish the letter in my voice as your mind wanders to the tone of my sentence anatomy.

Love is a foreign place, consummated and sealed. The love of you is the exact same as the love of me.

Marvelous Utopia

This can't be life. Calm waters rest as a light breeze wrestles through the limbs and leaves of the trees. Birds fly without flapping their wings rapidly. They soar along, engulfing the air in their lungs. The school of fish in shallow waters learns the navigation of the lake. The sun warms the beach without a brutal temperature. The sands warm bare feet that walk to enjoy the scenery within the confines of this marvelous utopia. Wildlife stays tame as they find peace within the human species and their interaction.

Unimaginative to view a setting so collectively serene, I sit and analyze as I shake my head from the perception of life being totally in place. The clouds never ordained the sky, so the beauty of the astrosphere ocean is visible for my thoughts to swim. My eyes serve as my pen as they write my heart's appetite in the sky, which I call, "Heaven's Lake." My smile is radiant, for its essence is the warmth felt by the coming and going of people I interact with daily. My eyes twinkle, like a flickering star in the blackened sky. My wonders today are released like doves trained to report to Heaven's doorstep.

I feel some type of way these days, like wording that was never created to explain my expressions or emotions. If my heart could speak to existence, it would blueprint values of morals and ethics to apply during your search for destiny. Blessings now have an unconditional presence to fulfill the voided gaps of exiled things given up for their arrival of new contents. Alone, I analyze and release it to my Father for approval. He has handcrafted my answers from prayers, and delivered testimonies to my soul to speak loud and clear on the subject matter.

Sculpted and massaged, is His gift to me with tailor-fit placement, which inserts into my life like the rib that vacated Adam's body. Today, the patience starts as I allow life to live through me, meticulously enjoying the resurgence of love, yet honoring and adoring all things conceived by Heaven. How long it takes for my Father to complete the task of sending a sealed approval weighs heavily on my faith. Faith I have plenty of, for my faith shows a side-by-side ceremony. Two individuals will be surrounded by the Spirit, remote from the onlookers that watch from a distance. As we consummate our vows, our Father will gather our hands in His and smile. A shepherd of choice will instruct us to kiss, and the tears that fall will now irrigate our seed planted. We sign the covenant with the sharing of one breath in two lungs. "This can't be life!" I initially thought. But it is. The essence of my domain I reside in now only has room for one. That one releases sunlight into my world that neighboring universes feed off of to warm their planets.

Addicted

I'm addicted to love, addicted to life. I'm obsessed with perfection, seeking life's treasures to obtain the perfect wife. From these treasures, I shall bestow upon her the riches of my planted seeds. Atypical to regular men, I hear her wants and carry out her specific needs. Addicted to her frame, her name and the intricate parts. Attached to her soul, her meaning, her role in my life to protect my heart. Maybe it's the strong angelic features in her facile cast. Or maybe it's the perfect lift of her cheek bone as she smiles, then her ensuing laugh. The look of her lips appears soft to touch and warrants my kiss. This magnifies my addiction as she closes her eyes and leans forward to insist. Taller than she, she soaks her head into my chest whenever we embrace. I tilt my head down every time to plant a forehead kiss, transitioning any expression on her face.

Her walk away is sensual, worthy of one's eyes to be mesmerized. The way she sashays is devilish, as if for me she was customized. Maybe it's the way her hips fit into my small hands or the arch in her vertebrae. Maybe it's her natural scent, her essence and how she forever wants to be under me. I could be addicted to the cartilage that makes up her ears, infatuated with running my tongue around and through as I whisper, "I'm yours for the remainder of my years." I have to believe it's the strong connection of passion we share. The abundance of oxygen, yet we thrive to share the same air. The way the water and conditioner curls her hair follicles, especially the way the water beads off her body that makes me so volatile.

I'm thinking it's the fact that her breast is a mouth full for me to caress. The way she grabs the back of my head as I move around the areola and nipple to release her stress. Addicted to making her legs shake uncontrollably, I set my goal to do that every chance she gives me. I love the fight she gives me to give back the giver, the long enduring gauntlets we have that elapses time, causes cold sweats, and earthquake magnified quivers. I know it's the waves in her derriere as I thrust from the rear. The way she bites her lip as she tries to look, pleasure cries I see the tear. The "I want you. I know you want me, too." The yelling and scratching, the biting as she screams, "This belongs to you." So I am addicted to her height, addicted to her size. I'm addicted to her beauty, mesmerized by her eyes. I am addicted to it all, the completion of the package. Definitely the shared love, in reality to anointed magic!

Tropical Storm

It rained inside my house today. My bedroom was soaking wet. The precipitation that caused the flood wasn't like anything I've ever seen before. I floated away in the essence of something unthinkable; to witness it still has me processing the unbelievable. I held on to my bed, gripping the spindles as the rapids rode me. The current was strong. The motion left the bed rocking in directions that almost caused me to submerge. The high waters drenched my sheets. I lay there, helpless, like a shackled prisoner waiting to be freed.

The fans sent breezes, yet the circular motion felt like high winds. The climate shifted, my body temperature elevated, and my brow started sweating. The constant struggle with me and the mini hurricane went on for several quarters, if not hours. My body held on, taking all that the storm gave. I spoke to it. She listened, but played with me. I wouldn't concede and it poured more into the wrath of beautiful destruction. I fought back, going against the current that pounced on top of me and struck back with unexpected movements. I changed the equilibrium and took matters into my own hands. As it poured a running river on me, I dug my paddle deep into the river and fought the current.

The storm enjoyed it, though the tone was less aggressive and more pleading. I was in the eye of the hurricane. I could visualize the break in the sky and see the light. The movements of my paddle, the gripping of the spindles, coupled with the warm waters of the rain. The echoes of movement, the cancellation of time, along with the fatigue of the storm had it drawing to a close.

Faster, I rowed. The deeper I pushed forward with my oar, the deeper the storm dug into my chest. As the storm hit the mainland, the yells proceeded. I yelled and so did the storm. The realization had cum and, together, we were exhausted. She broke the levies and flooded my city. She poured wet water on a summer day that shackled me to my bed. I lay there as the storm rode me, flooding my bedroom with the waters of avalanche of love-making. Sheets wet, body soaked, and the souls of two flooded with ecstasy.

I Stole…

It was a robbery, the stealing of a gift that was supposedly locked away. Yet the lock was open, and the gateway to obtain this theft was an open breezeway. I walked right in, well aware of the ramifications if I entered with my curiosity. This might not be right, but the wrongness of this act has me somewhere else during this heist. I'm in a warm place. The atmosphere is crisp from the inhaling and exhaling of my wind. The climate is appealing. My body temperature is rising as my blood rushes from the rush.

I feel her presence, like a soft breeze on my neck. I feel some type of way. The insides are confined. I interiorly decorate her floor plan to expand her opening, making it more comfortable to get in and out the tight space. I wash her walls, completely cleaning the structure with a "lick the bowl clean" attitude. The sun needs to shine in. I peruse through the midsection of the home to open a window once nailed shut by her. I rip the so-called curtains back. I finally get the window open after several body shaking pushes. The home gets drenched. Her carpet is wet as I maneuver through the flood.

For some reason, I feel her footsteps. Her heels walk on my back as her legs seem to be choking my torso. I'm wrestling with her furniture. I feel teeth prints on my neck and chest. I'm searching for her jewelry box--that valuable treasure has to be around here somewhere. My eye is red. I bump into those spit-shined walls from the one-eyed vision. It's getting wetter in here; the window is raining. I'm feverishly sweating, and the walls are dripping. I hear faint voices. They are distant, but I can make out the words. I can feel the homeowner about to cum. She utters curse words with deep sighs. I move through faster, holding on to whatever I can secure as I dig deeper for that buried treasure. She knows I am here. I can tell by the yells, cursing and asking the Lord for help.

The yelling won't stop! I move faster as I feel the top of the treasure box. I hear her panting! I wrap my hands around it as she grabs my back. She tries to speak as I open it for the first time ever, but the vocal cords are too late compared to my movements. The top came off. The treasure is exposed. The essence of beauty has now poured into her domain. I was engulfed, wet from rigorous perspiration, searching for that jewel. She looks in the eyes of her robber, shaking her head as her body shakes in disbelief.

Her eyes were almost bloodshot, along with teeth prints on her bottom lip. With nails in my back, I looked in my victim's eyes. I abused her home by knocking down walls and turning over furniture to remodel with my presence. That once open breezeway is now swollen closed. That light in the window is now blocked by curtains that sealed the outside. Her warm place left her in a cold sweat along with exhausted lungs. I have nothing more to do, but leave on my part from the violation. I stole something from her that wasn't mine. She left the door open, and I took what she didn't know could be given all at once. It was the perfect heist of the perfect home. I broke into her open house and stole her mind, body and soul! I leave her, nestled in her fetal position. She lay there with a smile.

Crescent Moon

She came in my doorway, standing in front of a crescent moon, seductively ready to pounce on me like prey. I shook my head and smirked. She took a deep sigh, rolled her eyes, and started stripping.

I watched her every movement with eyes of a hawk. She rolled her shirt over her chest. Her breasts popped up and jiggled as they repositioned themselves into correct posture.

She unbuttoned her pants, and I witnessed as the rest of her hourglass shape unveiled itself, with every centimeter headed south. She never took her eyes off me, enticing my vision with something she knew I wanted.

Pants to her ankles, I started to feel blood rushing to the tip of my wayward head. The man I was becoming was the man she wanted.

Victoria was holding the secrets that I wanted her to whisper all over me. She took two steps to get out of her pants. I took two fingers to unsnap her bra as she leaned forward. I used both hands to run my palms down her legs. Dropping her panties to the floor, I stared at the gap between her legs--silhouetted in the moonlight as she stood upright.

She pushed my forehead back, insisting on me lying on the floor. I graciously obliged. Straddling me, she rode my midsection till she felt it hit something connected to a deeper part of her womb.

She turned her body around to look out the open front door. She repositioned herself and grabbed her so-called friend that made the crease under her breast sweat. She gently massaged her friend and arched her back to lean forward for the gateway into her heaven to open into ecstasy. As she inserted the tip inside her, and before the deep breath she took, she spoke, "Such a lovely moon tonight."

Looking at her from the backside, I became mesmerized by the waves in her derriere. Sinking my ship further into her, she wet my legs with high waters trickling down my inner thighs.

As her cheeks split with each stroke, her heart-shaped ass hugged every inch of my curved midsection. Her back curved, her hair resting on her back as the follicles glued themselves to her skin from sweat of an erotic night.

Panting and cursing, she stared at that crescent moon, rolling her hips till the grey clouds covered the sky. Slapping her backside with my palm on each turn, with each separation of her ass, I was gradually losing control. The blood reached its point. Staring at her full moon, I gripped her waist, feeling her pelvis digging deep into me. With my nails on her hips, I released inside her and felt all I had scatter inward, like startled bats blinded by the light.

In the cool breeze of a steamy night, a crescent moon met a full moon and connected as one.

Titanic Ballroom

He sits on a park bench, centralized in the heaviest congested portion of the esplanade. It's like his body is exhausted, faint and weary from the road he walks. A simple resting stop now has become a reflection point pivotal to his essence. His posture is slumped, elbows on his thighs, as he focuses straight ahead. Gazing forward with an understanding of how his life shifted, he grips his warm libation with both hands to take a drink. He is reflecting on his curse, analyzing his gift.

The ability to engulf a room with his aura without uttering one word has him and his encounters amazed. Yet an outlook on life cultivates their mind to see clearer. If he converses through scribe, his words pop off the pages like short stories looking for a casting call. Positions, they seek, while the onslaught of navigating souls tries to leech onto his shell. They look for any warm spot they can sink their fangs into, praying their venom will paralyze his single status and warrant a connection to build a relationship. He is misunderstood, mentally advanced with depth unreachable for the current scuba teams, who are fishing for the geological find he calls a soul.

Sometimes he shortens the distance; he allows them to reach his vessel to canvas the treasure. The time frame they dwell around the confines belongs to their allotted oxygen that they prepped their equipment with to breathe. The water pressure isn't friendly. The skilled understand there may be alternative air pockets where they can gain extra supply. The breath they used to get down was manufactured and limited; the natural and heavenly breath will rescue and carry them through the remainder portion of the trip.

Once committed and willing, he removes their masks and kisses their lips as his breath fills their lungs. Some have been able to accept the oxygen like inhaling "a breath of fresh air." Others choke and swim back to the surface for the rescue crew to process the data. Deeper inside the confines, he takes the worthy. Inside rooms appeared locked and off limits. Down corridors and through suites, they travel. Artwork on various walls depict his inner dealings of life lived. In amazement at some portions of his life, a few concentrate their focus only in that section, causing them to break away from the rest of the pack.

He has navigated few people deep into the insides of his jeweled ship. Many have tried to remedy their lives by trying to run this marathon tour with him, but only trained mentally and spiritually for a sprint. Last door, last entrance to the one room that portrays his burning desire. Hopefully, one still stands, as he never looks behind him for clarity. Gigantic cherry wood, French, Tiffany-stained windows reflect light into an array of beautiful prisms on the floor of his hallway. He stands in front of the opening and takes a deep breath as he turns the handle and slowly pushes the doors open. The room is illuminated with a golden hue, which is strikingly stunning, like the other side of the Pearly White Gates.

He finds himself mesmerized every time he enters, overwhelmed by the positioning of everything his imagination has created and brought to life. The music plays as the chandelier dims for the mood. He extends his left hand and awaits the placement of a connection from the award-winning lady. As his arms hover for minutes, hoping that there is someone left who is in awe from the room, he realizes that there wasn't anyone to make it through the mental tour that ended in the core of his soul. No one again has fit the bill. Once again, he is forced to resurface to dwell landside to find what he searches for. On the park bench, he rests his body from the physical workout of the deep dive into his mental psyche. He focuses on the blue skies and envisions his soon-to-be heaven. In the midst of the busy and dreamless people, he prays. As he sits, she sits. As he looks, she turns. As he speaks, she smiles. As he wonders, she dreams. As he contemplates giving up, she gifts him with hope. As he thanks God, he closes his eyes and finds himself inside the rooms and corridors, swimming for her titanic ballroom.

The One I Let Get Away

The mahogany L-shaped desk engulfs my posture as I sit in the high-rested office chair. The computer is on, yet there is no browsing, surfing or work being done. I'm lost in a state of reverie, lost in time with my eyes wide open. Yet, I have no sight. My mind marvels at remnants of memories, threshold thoughts that cause instant paralysis in the world I own. Seat tilted back, shoes pointed toward the floor, my left elbow rests on the desk as my thumb rests under my chin. My index finger lies on my cheek bone, with my middle finger slightly bent above my top lip, but below my nose. One deep breath and I'm swirling. Funneling thoughts show images of skeletons buried in open view--constant reminders of how impactful a hold on your past affects your subconscious self.

Happy to be stretched, the old bones of the aged release fluid from the sacs of the joint to lubricate during choreography. I embrace the enchanted time, holding the ponderings close to my heart as I allow them to sink their head into my chest. Each limb makeup is that of an eventful time, years in correspondence, and dates on calendars that mark events that only have meanings to us. They are jelled with the emotions of yesteryear's dealings. Time ticks as the world in which I dwell progresses. I hear my voice speaking to break the tie. Something has me here. My ears are condemned from reasonable logic. My dormant shell shuts down, but the unconscious state forces me to believe I am growing from the love of old.

I caress would-be muscles in the back of the skeleton. The fibers in my fingers ease the pain caused by previous dealings. I want to show I can love and love better than I have in the past. I lift the head up and stare into would-be eyes. Like a reel in the theater, I see the days of togetherness come full circle--joyous times bound by unbreakable connectivity to man's deceitful strains on life. I blink, and then I close my eyelids. Leaning my head forward, I kiss the would-be lips of a mate that retracts the air in my lungs, bring me to my knees with collapsing organs. Beautiful to sight, magnificent in posture, and exhilarating in time spent--all the things that either cloud the thinking or give sight to see into the heavens. The dormant outside body is losing feeling. The comfortable pose that has one nestled in the seat is slipping. Muscles relax and pointed toes inch from perpendicular to parallel.

The voice of reasoning gets louder as it cracks the foundation that has sealed up my ears. Both arms pull tighter. Heads realign to force the lips back into perfect position. Eyes are closed during the lasting affection planted amongst the two. As eyes open, I, the dreamer, hold in his hands a few bones while others lie disassembled on the ground. The thoughts of past affections are now deceased as reality sets back in. The toes slip at a faster pace; the feeling of drifting takes over the dreamy wonderland. As the toes lose their connection, a jolt is felt and the swirl is back. There is an instant replay of all things seen in the enchanted moment, like a fatal glimpse of life. Coming to with a rapid heartbeat and opened eyes, the stares of reality are upon them. The cerebral hold is broken and the instance is no more. Yet, nothing felt so real, smelled so good, or warmed the heart like the joining of the one that got away and the time in life they captured in love.

Deferred Feelings

I should have been honest with her. Hell, I should have been honest with *myself*. I was in love with a woman that was in love with me. I mean, I was in relations with a woman that loved to have relations with me. Wait! I was in love with a woman that lay in a separate bed. I was in love with a woman that lay on another man's arm nightly, which served as her pillow. I stared at the moon and stars, at the ceiling and moving lights from passing cars, listening to the minutes of life tick away. I longed for her as another woman lay on my chest. I slept with restless thoughts, waking to yesterday's hold that she left on my heart.

We used to soak together in our moments. Her touch on my body was more than ecstasy on our lustful planet we inhabited. She felt secure with my arms wrapped around her. I felt the completion of self as she sunk her head into my chest and relaxed from life's infringements. Her imperfections were the characteristics that made her the one-off beauty I dreamt about.

She was his woman. Yet, she was my girl. I was her man, but someone else's property. We carefully executed every small window of opportunity into a full-blown theatrical love scene. She was the crutch that held me up. I was the smile that lit up rooms when she melted the boys' hearts with her presence. The first time I saw her froze my life. The first time I saw her, beauty walk past and smiled with a charisma that made me inquire. I knew she had me. As I spoke and she spoke back, I extended my hand to introduce myself. That's when I saw his diamond protruding off a setting, screaming engagement.

I daydreamed about her. Casual conversations connected us to life where our adolescence morphed. Same inner-city story, same relationship with a side of a city we both left behind in order to succeed. We talked from time to time about the relationships we were in. She took notes as I took score. Conversations grew as friendship blossomed. We never lied to one another. Honesty was our only policy. So honesty entered on a summer night. She stood in front of the headlamps of my car. A silhouette of a frame molded from heavens paved a walk of gold. The heavens had been good to her.

The first time I touched that man's fiancée, I came with the intent to make love to her better than any man she'd ever had. I succeeded. The first time I kissed his woman passionately, I did so with closed eyes as a chill shot through my body. The first chance she got to be held by the other woman's man, she nestled into his muscles and found refuge. The first chance she got to break the monotony, she laid back and let me speak to her body's language, speaking fluently on every conversation.

Days turned into months, as months turned into years. We were committed to the chase, driven by the taboo attraction we possessed. We went our separate ways eventually, left our love in her grandma's house with locked memories and unspoken emotion. I got a call the other day

33

from a friend that still had a good portion of my heart in her custody. I met up with her because of the weary voice she conveyed. When I saw her, it was the same beauty that was sealed away behind that locked door years prior. She wore the same smile with an aged wrinkle on the side of her mouth. Not much changed—it was the same personality, same physique and same mystic that made me fall in love with her years ago.

Last night, I hugged that man's wife, and she wrapped her arms around me, lying on my chest. Last night, she lifted her head and ran her cheeks against mine, taking a deep breath and letting the memories flow through her veins. Last night, she stared deeply into the face of another woman's priority. As we looked past each other's pupils, down into the souls that held emotions that had been locked away for so long, I watched her tear up.

Last night, I kissed the soul of hidden emotions with my lips, and she kissed back. Last night, I kissed the lips of another man's wife that needed love because he told her he didn't love her anymore. Last night, she kissed the lips of another woman's property like she never wanted to let go. Last night, we stopped lying and told the truth about the feelings we deferred for so many years. Last night, we broke away from reality and lusted for the love we once had.

Unspoken Intentions

She opened the door, draped in the coziest nightwear. Her hair was pulled to the back, but not quite yet formed into a ponytail. She sashayed from the door to the chair, leaving her wanted guest at the door to secure the promises. Walking past her, he slowed down, anticipating her actions would release a sign of affection in the form of a kiss or a hug. Yet, nothing transpired. He sat alone on the couch, confusingly watching television. Looking at her frequently, he detected an eerie aura.

Now well into the night, the purpose was to hold each other affectionately until daylight graced the windowpane. Yes, they've been down this road before. Gazing into the ceiling, he wondered if he made the right decision to come over.

Tired from a long day, he prompted the direction of the evening to migrate to the bedroom. Without speaking, she gripped the remote, turned the television off and rose from her seat.

As the walked down the corridor leading to the steps, he admired her perfect shape. Her beauty mesmerized him; every inch of her was chiseled to his perfection. He forecasts the evening highlights mentally and awaits for the prime opportunity to showcase his affection through lust and love for her, to her.

Still leading the way, her face still housed the same grim an uncertainty, which he couldn't decode.

The room was chilled from a window fan that projected the autumn night into the room. She slid under the covers as he rested outside her self-made cocoon. They exchanged minimal words as he placed a passionate, yet sensitive forehead kiss between her eyebrows. Her eyes closed as she took in the feeling, inhaled his scent and relaxed as he ran his hands through her wavy hair.

Chit-chat turned into laughter as they found a reoccurring experience to ease the mood. Her mind suddenly relocated the thought that subdued her face into the back of her mind, pushing it to the point of no return. His job is to make sure sweet slumber is met, and met by any means necessary.

As the laughter got louder, he entertained the gag with a bright smile, but the softest of eyes. She lay on her back to allow the departure of her cozy nighttime outfit. He continued his joke, using his teeth as scissors to snap a plastic piece that hung from her panties.

Gentleman-like, he acted as though he was going to place them back on her body, but opted to pass. Sliding both legs through the holes of the undergarments, he dived face down between her legs. Kissing and touching her in the right spots, her body convulsed and released the purist irrigation known.

She instructed him up toward her, rubbing slowly and digging her nails into his back. He lost his bottoms as she moaned and whispered sensual fits of passion. Piercing her moist lips made her back bend as he slowly progressed. Her nipples stiffening, the erotic passion of lovemaking commenced.

Unaware of the time and exhausted from thrusting and bending, the two lay next to one another, staring deeply into each other eyes. Time ticked and they both fell deeply into a comatose state. Waking up startled, he checked the clock. Leaving her sound asleep and fully content, he let himself out.

As he approached his office the next day, he knew a twisted turn was right around the corner. Slowly, he read a letter which stated, "I need a favor. I need you to walk away from this relationship."

Baffled by the discovery, he immediately understood why. With the cards stacked against him, he agreed to the written request. Though the hurt inside ate at him, he wore his pain well; he maintained his charismatic demeanor.

He detached himself from work and hid in his emotions as he drove home. Reflecting on the recent chain of events, he grew agitated by her actions after they consummated relations of divine order. He only wished for an answer, wishing she would reconsider the declaration to at least let him show her it was more about love than lust.

His heart cried as his mind tried to jokingly point the finger in her direction. They were equally guilty of the relationship, bonded together without a solid foundation. He commended their efforts and silently wished her well. He hoped by doing so it would draw a common denominator they could plant and nurture.

As he prepared to ask her, no words could bring a smile or happiness back at this point. Begging to depart with a promise to communicate, she left the conversation before he uttered a word.

Loneliness entered as his night became mortified from the lack of his companion. He became star-struck and prayed that she, too, had it as rough as he did. He wanted to be that pillow she held tight. The tip of the finger that wiped the tears away. The sheets that she wrestled with all night as she lingered on their past relations. He just wanted *her*.

He cried that night, for the departure of his goddess was now true. She entered his life with a timestamp that expired with his departure from her room that night. She reached out for him to stay, but thinking routinely plagued his mind. The pillow on which he rested his head now became the pillow that absorbed his tears of sorrow.

Morning After

She feels some type of way today. The sun beams on her a certain heat that rises her body temperature. Far from the perspiration that induces the sweat glands to rage into a sprinkler system, her insides move, yet she sits still. The mind that controls the neural system lingers into a realm of sexual desires. Uncontrollable to resist, she plays around with the thoughts, allowing them to wrestle in erotic positions, compromising the seated position she resides in. Unbearable is the lack of breathing she has inserted into her lungs. That breath of fresh air is needed, and she needs to locate it. Pausing to maintain what is left of her composure, she shakes her head and tries to locate a remedy. Instantly, she locates her cell phone and texts a friend, fingers moving quickly. Yet, she uses limited words. The message reads that of a persistent woman: *"I want to have sex!"*

The flip side of the spectrum is a man who is caught off guard by the message finding. He dwells on the previous occurrences and knows that the friendship is severed, yet intact, if the path of abstaining from one another is executed immediately. He weighs his schedule. It's a little past high noon and the bills don't get paid if he leaves work. Just one more time, he wants to knock a dent into the psyche of his friend. The problem is the roughness of the two once they encounter the pure nakedness of their fames.

Both single in their right, one has a situation that is a little more delicate. Timing is everything, so they play around with when and where. The interaction has a deadline of 5 p.m., three hours from now. They analyze the problems, devising a fool-proof plan.

After careful litigation between the two, he packs up his work station and heads out the back door of his building. She wraps up her work and walks out the front door with a mission, vision illuminating on her face. As they drive, they converse lightly. Everything is set, yet the contraceptive is missing. She regains her feeling, but doesn't keep condoms handy. The meeting place is her house, and his rubbers are at his house. Too much to change the venue, they agreed to disagree on this one.

Since she is closer to the store, she purchases the needed item for the event. Her initial shock was the price gauging of the utensils. A mere three-pack costs $3. She now fabricated the reasoning that there are so many kids--lack of money to purchase birth control. He instructed her on everything from the brand to the size.

They met at her house. He is there first. She pulls up and heads to the front door, opening the doors to her home. He walks in after her, looking at her sex appeal to guarantee that the act is comfortable with his state of mind.

It's been a couple of months since the last happening. The previous outing was epic, complete with hickeys on necks, scratches on his chest, a sore pelvis on her part, and carpet burns on multiple limbs for the both of them. This time, they needed ground rules. This time, they probably needed a referee. If this was going to be the last time, they would have to go harder than before.

Casual conversation ensued, as they caught up face-to-face to break the tension in the room. As they talked, she unbuttoned the top button of her pants. She picked up the plastic grocery bag that contained the necessary party favors. She seductively fed him instructions: "Time to get undressed."

His ears don't deceive him, and the indication helps promote blood flow to his key component. She watches as he releases clothes off his body, like a strip tease. She sinks in her seat as he exposes the chest she loves to kiss, lay on and massage. Before his pants drop, he reaches for her hand and escorts her to the bedroom, finding refuge in the bed she rests in solo nightly.

The honor of undressing her is his pleasure. She allows him to snatch the garments off and throw them into a pile. The bed sits high up, so the elevation is just right for the act at hand. As he drops his boxers to the floor, she lifts her head to look at the friend she missed so much. His right hand instantly pushes her head back onto a pillow it rested on during the undressing.

He rolled his tongue from her left kneecap around the pelvis, to stop at the opposite knee. She tingled while he licked around her. He knows what it is that will cause her to skyrocket. He planned to send her mentally into outer space.

41

His tongue graced her inner thighs. Before she could utter a word, her exposed vertical lips are met with his. His tongue is finely engineered in carving out the insides of delicate finding. That is his course for the night.

Her body arches, with her butt rested on the side of the bed. The only thing else touching it is the back of her slightly raised help. She squeals and moans as she tries to maintain her composure. Unfortunately, that left her with the connection of his taste buds against her inner walls. If this bed were a track, the race was already won once the gun went off.

She shook feverously as the temperature in the cool room hit her body thermostat, catapulting it to inferno hot. She knew she stood no match, but pleasure like this isn't common. For uncommon things, she was willing to sacrifice. With her last little bit of dignity, her sexual juices raced out like the Gulf of Mexico flooded into New Orleans once the levies broke. The erotic seizures and constant gripping of the sheets left her muscles fatigued. To top it all off, the insertion of his gold member hadn't even happened yet.

She curled up like a fetus with no womb to protect her. The first feat was now complete, but the second was grounds for a firework display during Independence Day. While he allows her a few seconds of rest to place the sexual hat on, he surveyed his subject. He grips her left leg and swings it over to line her back parallel to the bed. She is vulnerable and he knows it. This was her doing, her wanting, but it was his finishing.

He glides up her frame with a destination of the right-side area of her neck, kissing around her lower ear and collarbone. She shook from the intimate touch, gripping his back with her soft hands. Familiar with her private area and in tune with his delicate pointer, he pierced the lips with ease.

Unprepared for the act, simply taken off guard, she sinks her nails into his back and bites his neck. Smaller than him, she is engulfed by his size, both in her midsection and in life. His physical frame is riddled with muscles. She admires his hard work to maintain the chiseled shell.

The standard missionary stance is present for only a few moments. He then un-wraps her legs from around his back, stretching them out to form a V-shape for greater penetration. She pushed against the wall as she yelled, sorry for whatever it is she has done. Her breathing is choppy. Her head is against the wall and her frame configures a C-shape. "Wait! Wait!" These seem to be the only words she can muster up. It's clear who's in control. Vulnerable to the lack of muscular ability, she is at his mercy.

He spreads her legs wide, pressing them against the bed. She somehow repositioned her head off the wall to gain greater comfort. With her ankles at her ears, her tailbone is lifted off the bed and her eyes are somewhere in the back of her head. As he climbs up on her hamstrings, she swings her hands, trying to push him backward. She misses the desired objective because something feels like it is being tampered with in her ovaries. Her fallopian tubes close up as he thrusts in and out at a moderate rate.

He rolls her on her side and splits her legs for a side entrance. The new position causes her to reach again for a central object to grip. He penetrates her inside at a rate that should govern a speeding ticket. He slaps her on her ass as she tries to collect her breath. He runs his hands up her chest to caress her breast. She is flabbergasted, but unavailable to comment on the pleasurable abuse she is experiencing.

She sinks her head into the mattress as he repositions her bottom half and lifts her midsection. Resting on her knees, she asks, "What are you doing to me?"

He leans forward while dislocating his valuable out of her on purpose. Sensually, he says, "Trying to be the best you ever had!" That was enough to send her body into convulsions.

He licks down her spine, as she begs for more time. It's too late. He was head-first back inside of her, with his tongue touching somewhere close to her cervix.

She yelled, "What the fuck!"

He licked and caressed as her body, allowing her midsection to speak to him loud and clear.

His work was almost complete. All he needed to do was release a galactic rush into the condom, blowing it up like a balloon full of air. Something clicked in him. Today, he wanted her to get it out, to ride it like she was buckled down on top of a bull at the rodeo.

She sat on top of him, slowly inserting his third leg into her womanhood. She bent forward as he described her insides as having extra area that she never knew existed. She slowly rolled her hips, scratching his chest as her hair flipped back and forth. She bounced up and down faster as she rode the horse attached to him like the final turn at The Derby.

He looked down as he heard her noises getting closer, like contractions. She released all over him, her insides wetter than a Seattle rain. She cursed, screamed, shook and pleaded for him to release as she rung her internal doorbell several times.

He felt the sensation. He wanted his hammer to hit her insides at the right moment to skyrocket her. As she grinded back and forth, the bell inside of her left her lower half paralyzed. He stiffed up his legs and warned her to prepare for blast off. She listened and tapped her insides with force as the two exhaustedly skyrocketed at the same time. On top of him, breathing heavily, she shook in a cold sweat. They passionately kissed to seal the deal.

Their mission now complete, they could now go back to being friends, with nothing but lust separating them. As she lifted up, she instantly yelled. He looked down at his midsection to see a bare remnant of his body that he covered prior to the act. The device had to be severed while she was on top and now was lodged inside her. Surgery had to be performed, as he searched her insides like an OBGYN. Minutes went by. He knew that if he gripped it the wrong way, the condom would filter into her system and swim for her egg. Finally finding it, he analyzed its contents. With his juices still nestled in the plastic, he breathed a sigh of relief at first.

As they stared at each other, they knew this was lust--nothing more, nothing less. They opted for the over-the-counter remedy. It was an act that had to be done. It was the morning   after.

Interference/Distraction

His mind wanders frequently. He knows his spouse, so the small movements of distance lately have him questioning the relationship stance. He's older these days, so his mind tells him that he has been down this road before. He feels like even if he hasn't endured it in life, his knowledge of such is helpful enough. As the demons plague his cranium, his life becomes consumed with the best avenue of action to take. Scared for the results, he hesitates to formulate a game plan.

They say the best thing in a relationship is communication; but talking when you want to accuse is far from the best conversation with your mate. She is witty. If things aren't outlined in proper format when asked, she will devour his passiveness with treacherous responses. From this, he knows that a sword in a long-distance gun fight isn't an option. He regroups, slowing his mind down to justify why things have taken a turn in recent days. Lunging back into the committed portion of the union, he believes that, with time, the problem will disappear. Little does he know that the issue isn't from the time lapse they don't spend, but rather from the time immense prior to his existence with a helpful stranger.

This breach has historical bearings of monumental ranks. Thought to be dead and buried, it has now done the unthinkable and resurfaced like a team of archeologists, bringing the Titanic out of its watery grave. She stays as cool as a polar bear with his nails dug into the ice. She'll never display the cards in her hand. She would rather cut the arms off the opposing player to gain leverage. Her man's spider senses are looming large. He asks probing questions, but the taunting is becoming disrespectful. He hears or sees nothing from her side, yet the fight song echoes vigorously in his mind. On her toes at all times, she feels the goose bumps on her neck, like a soft kiss between her ear and collarbone. One of them has to take a stand. Where he is feeling left out and confused, she is mesmerized by the heat from sweet serenades that have entered into life lately. Far from indulging in the charismatic charm that comes with the sweet sounds, she paces herself to fully indulge in what has been constant.

Though the melodies tickle the eardrums, just as the words of written scribes roll her eyes to the back of her head from their placement in sentence patterns, she knows that insecurities come and go. The ability to waltz like her man can leave her breathless several times weekly. If questioned, honesty couldn't be an option. Answering in that manner would be as much of a death blow as the rock that left David's slingshot that killed Goliath. Recently, his nights are spent sleeping a little more. Although his thoughts play leap frog, he understands that sleeping is the playground for thoughts created and killed over time. To hold a commitment with another person is a sacrifice. You give away your protective covering of your heart to another individual in hopes that they will forever protect it. As days pass into weeks, the sounds of music in her ear won't fade, but gets lowered to smaller decibels. The words seen through writing will scale back their prolific painting style in order to allow her to see a clear view of reality. From this, hopefully the reluctance on his part will diminish. Hopefully, it doesn't grow into a thorn in the side of their spirited association.

She knows at any given moment, just like a track runner with the sound of the gun, the music can cue along with the dialogue writings that have held the attention of her. She doesn't know that the writer's poems have infinite syntax when it comes to love, and the composition of the symphony is a never-ending assortment of blissful spiritual chimes, if ever fully anointed with the opportunity to unite.

Her Intentional Distance

Indifferent is the term that clothes my heart. This so-called union isn't making sense to me. It was all good just a week ago. The time doesn't seem that long ago. Joyous interactions make me smile, but I need more than a mere grin. The love of us might not be outlined the same in both of our eyes. What you see must not be what I see. We sit on a couch, in a room all alone. Yet, the distance feels like we're walking from coast to coast. We talk and you're staring through me. The words you speak are talking at me, not to me. When I need you, you're there. But the moments afterward, you check out. I'm in love with a corpse--a corpse that comes and goes with a soul.

Do you know what it's like to want to progress and the atmosphere surrounding you have you stagnated? This right here is killing me and causing a realistic nightmare. Maybe you know not what you do. Maybe there are deeper issues that might need to be addressed. The problem we address will probably fall on a wasted lot. There is an address, but no residence for delivery. I'm getting frustrated, weary of my thoughts running a marathon that I'm not able to complete. Emotionally, I'm drained. Mentally, you're gone. Where is the happy median? I know I pushed--pushed you toward greater goals and away at times. I've closed myself off to the world and you tried to give me just that. Hypercritically, I know. But never did I think that this would happen to me. You've done no wrong, yet this isn't right. There isn't any hate, yet we are lacking a ton of love. Distant interactions of lust give off falsified hope. I feel connected to you, but only when we are stuck together like animals. If I could live in that moment, I would forever. But the walls of my insides close in after the deposit of unsown seeds drown in my birth canal. I smile at you. Forgive me for these tears. But I'd choose rather not to die for you over the next few years. How about we take the good times, the friendship, and understanding, then mix it all together into one drink? We can get drunk off separation and just have memories forever.

Separation Before the Storm

She lays on me, her head in my lap, eyes closed with a smile--one she never had prior pasted on her face. She lets go with me and allows her first of many to occur. Her body is in love with mine; the connection is beautiful. I am a giver, so I give her what she thought people lied about having. The ecstasy that she now releases has her wondering what took so long for her to get me to come into her life. She is in Heaven. Her small touch of what love feels like has her holding on like she has one arm, her dangling body swinging off a high-storied building. Yet as she sleeps, my eyes hover over her and stare, looking at her weary shell. Her body is worthy, but my thoughts are clouded.

My life is sending me messages, as I slowly crack codes for understanding. She houses this space in my time, yet I really want to fade away. I softly stroke her hair back. The arched eyebrow, coupled with her angelic features, has me shaking my head in confusion. Not from disgust, but more from my mind's message. She is new to my life, and I'm not going to be able to weather my storm with others aboard. So I stare down as she feels our hearts connecting. I shake my head again, knowing she is a good woman. The timing is now wrong as I stare down these stormy coordinates. But my message is clear: I have to wipe all things away to receive this futuristic moment. Its days away, and I feel it burning my core of existence. My heart is clear. The next step is my soul and mind. I'm hugging and kissing to say goodbye. She is hugging and kissing to create tomorrow with us. It's amazing how the new directives come at any moment; they are sealed with the Lamb's blood.

She starts to wake. I look down as she rolls over to gain positioning. Her smile grows larger than the one she housed in her slumber. I smirk back, knowing goodbyes are hard to facilitate. As she sits upright, she leans and plants a warm kiss on my lips. I close my eyes to accept. All the time, I am praying for strength and the correct words that won't kill the new self-esteem she has been awarded. As I open my eyes, my face turns solemn. A deep breath and sigh follow shortly thereafter. Once my mouth opens, I am now preparing for battle of the soon-to-be disturbance. Some moments in life have no preparation; this is one of them. She stares with her piercing brown eyes. They melted me all our short days. Yet today, they hurt to focus on. My lips part as my mouth opens. The following is the beginning of the end. I utter, "We need to talk." She obliges the notion and redirects her posture. The conversation begins as the horizon's clouds darken on my skies!

The Pier

My shell sits planted in the last place we sat, the place where it was you and me, surrounded by warm air. Nestled in a patch of grass, we talked. There were so many questions that should've been answered, but weren't. Close to a cliff, the river water moistens the border rocks. We stare down at our reflection in the wavy current. It's our mirror into the present. Honestly, it's our portal back into the past. Together as one, yet one with a cracked foundation of love, pouring out into the atmosphere on which we stand. We walk down a planked boardwalk, holding the rails and slowly taking in the moment.

We're grown. We lived in a brief time period prior to conversing about the split second that damaged our once make-up. I admit. I have indulged in acts that tore sin into two, and then multiplied to become relational cheating. Man enough to discuss the act, I thought it could be handled. But the pill was too big to swallow. It was now a scared relationship with haunted relationship regurgitation of deceit and lies. We walk down the wooded path with no understanding of how we got there. Maybe the weight from our skeletons crushed the shoulders we both carried the world upon. Odd thing is our heads never drooped low. We kept eye contact directly with the face of our supposed soul mate. Reaching the farthest point, we rest, finding refuge in the sunset.

Gazing at the beauty, we focus, looking on at a city that we probably should've departed seven times over. Closely, we stand. Technically, we still belong to one another. Forehead kisses and tight hugs ensue. Departure has come as time catches up with us. Slowly walking back to that patch of grass, we find laughter. She stays ahead and I watch love walk out of my life, consistently asking for another opportunity, if it be God's will.

Nothing was resolved during that talk, yet the unmasked love we possessed showed itself. As long as she loves me, there's no need to ask the hard questions. I conversed with the Lord and He gave closure. She wasn't strong enough to furnish answers to the questions if presented. Days into months, calendar pages tear as years accumulate since the separation. I still go lose myself on that path of grass. I walk down that planked pathway at the same time of the day to watch the sunset over the city that still has my heart. Alone, I stand. Alone, I walk, but my heart changes not. Not one waver of repetition has occurred. The river shows my image as the city holds my heart. The Lord holds the allotment of time. I release my soul into the breeze off the river's current.

The Muted Gramophone

She loves him; her heart beats for his happiness. The admiration is in her eyes. Pictures silhouette love into thousands of words. She longs for his company; he is her boyfriend that vaults transgressions away for happiness. The lungs that share his air each time they kiss has collapsed. The atmosphere on Earth isn't sufficient for her to live. Life as she knows it is being sucked away at an unstoppable pace. If she could, she would cease the momentum. But it has a mind of its own.

The world views her life in seconds, and a public relations person can mastermind a cover-up. Yet, her covered heart that was once blanketed by him is exposed for all to see. If a cave could be found remotely tucked in some corner of the world, paparazzi would still lurk out the coordinates to snap photos of her broken existence.

He lived with a characteristic that was hidden for so long; a characteristic that he talked about vaguely while she held him during his descriptive outpour. A characteristic that she thought made him different because of his passion to never be like his past eyesight. A characteristic that she never thought would be unleashed onto her.

Mere conversation about God knows what turns into an argument that turns into world news. She yells as he yells. The two exchange their fiery personalities that wouldn't back down. The confines of a vehicle steam like smoke coming out the tailpipe of the Italian luxury bull that housed the dispute. The roaring engine of that bull was fast, but the stronghold of social media proved to be faster.

Blurred and speculative are those ensuing moments. Vague in description the two have been since the aftermath. They broadcast scripted addresses to the fans and the public with emotional longing for their love. The media posts facial shots to invite the pop princess into a spokesperson for the cause role, yet she just wants to speak to the person that was the cause alone. Lend a helping hand to the person that once whipped her tears away. Maybe find refuge in the same arms that own the fist that struck her repeatedly.

Nobody asked or understood their wants after the altercation. The judge issued the sentencing upon him. He accepted without a fight because of his wayward actions. Time is a double-edged sword that heals to cover wounds in which small scars are left for remembrance.

He loves her dearly. He hits high notes precisely in every rendition of love he sings, every lyric that is undertone for her; every still delineation that he goes back to for inspiration. Merely kids in the spotlight of the world's conniving eye. The industry was everything to the love connection within both of their stratosphere. He's from his commonwealth state, and she's from her island resort paradise homeland. Both were crowned royalty to elevate their genre.

The crossroad is now, presently presented as age shows their hearts' cry. Memories of the incident is there--no physical wounds, but mental in terms. Divided fans talk, but the growth of a strong woman makes an appeal that's distinguishing for the reconnection of friendship. A savvy approach to the resolution of love. Truly in love, she admits, as the world stares at their screen that projects her strengthened image. In love with self, comfortable finally in her skin, and purely in love with his love, she sighs as the questions end the interview finally.

When Night Falls

She is there, the place where the soul and mind evacuate. Yet the heart still has a faint beat that belongs with her covenant. Though weak in sound once listened to, it's big enough to allow time to pass and give countless allocation to the connection of her mate. Realistically, she has departed. Her shell lingers behind because of responsibilities they hold together. Strategically, she plots. Exit plans need to be precisely calculated when the clock strikes the departure moment. Useless arguments show that he is unfit to work harder than need be. He doesn't seem to understand that love isn't the only thing that holds a foundation together during relationships. Mere departures of materialistic hubbies can't help the void that has a strain on the wondering heart of hers.

You can't sell objects and expect the transaction to make you anew. The soul has to be cleansed with public displays of guilt as redemption meets disparity of fallen love. Her outside radiates a vibrant demeanor. Yet, her soul cries out for outlets to release the frustration of how so-called allowance brought situations to the forefront. He rests, for the life of old made immature moves that broadcasted his lack of full commitment to connected life. He didn't understand that his name could change several times over. Some for the good, some for the bad--in a split second. He went from single to boyfriend, boyfriend to fiancé, fiancé to husband, from husband to father. He went from father to liar, liar to cheater, cheater to adulterer. At the end of it all, he went from adulterer to divorced, with divorced leading back to singleness.

He understands not what to do or how to do anything to keep the latter from happening. Borrowed time seems to hover like dismal days with no blessings in sight. She holds firm to her positioning. Her shell is present, but leaves an absent connection of attractive measures. She holds out toward him. But really, she holds on to the few things that connect the two. Man must understand once deceitful the grail that spawns life after months of nurturing is eliminated from casual visits. The mess he made may not be repairable, so the closest he gets are the offspring the two made while the covenant was truly present. Her heart beats faintly as her soul drops the remaining connection on the streets he stepped out into, causing irreconcilable differences. The gavel has slammed, judgment to be awarded. Yet, to declare a winner is to honor the loss of time she thinks she wasted during their strained vows.

They...The Cheater

They hear not the heartbeat of their union. They hear not the cries of their created children. Far from the morals of their religious backing, they slide. They're light years away from their goals through sacrifice. They're closer to the curiosity of want. The focus of need is housed in a labyrinth of spiraling emotions. They walk out the door of a home in order to roam in the streets of misconception. They leave behind truth and stability to promote lies and sporadic moments. They cloud their minds up with meditated thoughts of sexual touches.

Passionate encounters leave the scent of destruction. They break the vows of love because the trust they have for self can't commit to the goal of unification. They long for another while in the company of their mate. Their mind formulates their hidden person's image frequently. Yet their lips catch the larynx vibrations before it calls out the wrong name. They battle with deception while they pray for the light. They hope nothing comes out the closet, so they barricade the door with nails and a dresser. They age in the face. The distress shows wrinkled facial features of a hard life birthed through lies. People notice slight changes in demeanor and scheduling, but they ignore it. The soul cries out, their hearts feel like they are stuttering. All they can do is watch through the body's distant eyes. Flashing renditions of less than an hour of deceit replays through split seconds of thoughts by falsified connection.

Their life is like the Portuguese that feared the world was flat, drifting on a memory. But really, the end of your world is near. The drop off the world is vicious, with a public viewing that is ferocious. The rain will come one day and flood their world without a rainbow to grace their sky. That devil had them do it, I guess. He made them take the truth out of their existence and lie. Yep, that devil made them take that ring off the left finger and get a hotel room. Made them make love to a stranger like they would die for their spouse's happiness. Taste the juices of their deceitful partners as they blocked their blessings. Lonely nights with moneyless pockets grace the realm of the cheater's domain. That same spouse they overlooked left, just like the person they laid down with once they wanted more than a wet ass. They gave it all to their fabrication of self, lied on life and the devil helped pave an avenue to travel. They thought the lifestyle was fabulous until they learned that the devil was a liar.

Jack the Ripper

She was left with lacerated tracks of pain from the tears I caused on her cheeks.

I looked in her face and saw the abandonment of hope I left her.

She looked at me as her beginning of her happiness.

I killed that thought, causing emotions that started the end of us.

I never meant to hurt her, but all men say that.

My deceit trapped her heart.

I took her kindness for weakness; I took her unconditional want to love as just talk, and not action.

She watched as I demolished her security wall, which was built to ward off predators like myself.

She watched as I unmasked her insecurities to wage war on her perception, vessel and spirit.

I infiltrated her intimate space with intentions and lies.

Leary in her thoughts, she gave trust to my serpent tongue as my lips moved with words.

Trusted my lips as my cold heart kissed her passionately.

She questioned my motives, only to mistake the words I answered with as the entrance of her prayer completion.

Never should a heart filled with so much joy plummet to the earth to shatter into unmendable particles.

Never should I feel any remorse toward the death of her soul that I killed while she entrusted it in my possession.

I made love to her in the steamy city fog; I bid her adieu under moonlight with the blood wrapped in her love on my hands.

Within Those Walls

Within those walls, the whisper of voices can be heard. They cast a pitch that releases old sorrows from lust lost in crevasses within the foundational cracks. They warn and plea for departure. Their souls are latched to the grail that cupped their milt.

Within those walls, the light is extinct. Murky and decrypted is the aura that kills the vegetation of monthly fruit. Lawless navigators stain imprints in hydrographic blood splatter for territorial markings.

Within those walls, the inches inserted into the journey felt like miles traveled. The distance from border to border is lengthy. Oh how the gap between love and lust has spread the legs of distance from confiding in so many all-seeing eyes.

Within those walls, the fertile roes break at irregular cycling. They burst suppress-filled emotions with an injection seeping destroyer, firing off in her incubator. The soul-wrenching quakes of gyrating encounters have the diffusing eggs bleeding out, penning a letter with only one line that says, "Dear life."

Within those walls, savages rampaged the temple of the queen. They encounter her kingdom and pillaged the holy treasure; they left false artifacts of hope for her swollen orifice. The shattering of her hymen particles are wrapped in tears from trampled tread marks where her sailors journeyed.

Within those walls, a woman screams out in her hidden pain. She rocks herself, holding her womb, weeping of birth with no seed.

Within those walls, the howls of men's souls outweigh the muffled noise of shallow esteem, searching for connection minus self-doubt.

Within those walls, a longing for love, the feeling of want, and the nurture of development all send tears to those once innocent eyes of this maiden.

Within those walls, a mausoleum of aborted birthrights is mourned by the to and fro kinetic power of heartless red-eyed men.

Walk Away Love

I cry as you cry. After today, we will not wipe away each other's tears.

Never have I wanted to admit this day could happen. Our separation is my worst fear.

We shielded each other from our nightmares; we vaulted away each other's transgressions.

Your secrets will not be uttered from my mouth. Promise me you won't release my confessions.

Our intimacy is now buried, deceased with a funeral to say farewell.

The two of us being sole survivors, the level of our once love we can never tell.

Nobody can insist to speak of our pros and cons. Our matured good times opposed to the bad.

Nobody lived in our world, but us. They can only be one-sided on what we once had.

Together, we once held hands. But today, I will let mine fall.

I will break my connection from this. The night's end will be the final curtain call.

The theatrical props are pulled. The cast bows, then your half shall exit left.

Mine shall be pulled right. One last glance and I mutter, "Be blessed."

The door to our house has now been closed. We relinquish the title and can never again call it home.

Your body can't lie next to me as we once slept in the sheets.

Of the bed that we bought together, your head on my bicep can no longer rest your cheek.

The outings are no more in the public eye that has crowned us as an adorable pair.

The consummated break-up of us has taken the fresh breeze and allowed smog into the air.

Sunny days lay down to let overcast skies remain dominant.

Our smiling faces showcase solemn sighs; we cry as the sky begins to precipitate.

Unfortunately, the things that caused us to fall in love have diminished

The book of our relationship is closing its cover. The novel is now sealed and finished.

The days will get long as the time moves ever so slow.

After we release our intertwined hearts into freedom, we allow them to re-grow.

Our memories, we have; but to dwell on the past is totally forbidden.

A silent event in our life, but we prepare for our days of independence.

One last hug, coupled by a pair of kisses.

I cry on the inside and wipe her eyes as I depart from my Mrs.

Prisoner of War

The ides of the month are heavy; they swarm moment after moment. The locus of effects spirals my life into an abyss darker than residency on the arctic ice sheets. I'm remotely positioned with a shell, minus an understanding soul. These problems I hold are my responsibilities. It's my life and my fate. The path I walked has no stumbling or road blocks--more like an ended road with a cliff that warrants a drop from a distant nebular to Earth's shallow ground. The free-falling momentum of my endeavors has me up, without sleep.

The calendar dates means nothing. The clock hits the same hours as I watch sunrise to sunset multiple times before my red eyes are blanketed by my eyelids. This can't be right. My heart is golden like the roads of Heaven. Yet I feel like asphalt as I get trampled by abusive pedestrians. I want my bed to smother me in its rectangular shape and ease my ailments back to perfect working order. Seems like I lay and hear all the noises of the universe through these ears-thumping sounds that screech a soundtrack to my current days. I need something--something that can take me into a spiritual coma to get away from this madness.

Acquisitions of me intentionally hurting and harming. Hell, I've been the victim for years. A drunken scheme to shatter my life into pieces too fine for reconnecting adhesive, has me plummeting. The loss of a career I love and personally wake up to do is hanging on a wet string that loses strength as my faith decreases. I gave too much power, should have confronted this personal problem years ago. Should have bonded one out and locked the other away as the invasion of my records was leaked for their personal gain, minus racketeering. But what do I do now? I'm screaming at self and I'm not vocally uttering a word. I laid hands on a person? Please! I broke through my breaking point and had enough.

Now look at this--charges of insane antics that even the mentally disturbed think are diabolical. I just want to pray and sleep, sleep and pray. Day after day, I'm constantly reminded. Day after day, I cry my soul's deepest bellow. I need something. The anxiety is becoming too much. Sleep is needed. I'm exhausting my mind. It's reading like a psychopath's brain waves when recorded by a therapist. I can remedy the circling thoughts with water and a bottle of sleeping pills. My eyes are red, along with a heart decreasing in warmth. The outside world is moving, while my inside world feels like it is halting. One pill, two pills and then, I lose count on purpose. I wonder if this will really help my cause to find rest from existence. I sway in my nestled position as I dream of genies to allow me three wishes. They must be working as I smile at nightmares of old. If I should die before I wake, then I pray the Lord my soul to take. My eyes close and I wrestle no more, comfortable in a fetal position. I feel like I'm back in the valley of the unborn, ready to get drafted to a new set of predecessors. My lungs are full of air. My heartbeat is steady. All while my muscles relax, I am finally at peace.

Rambling Screen Play

Here we go...

What the hell? Seriously, this is what we came to? No real communication, no unidentified sighting. This is the envisioned breakthrough? The yesteryears are erased and filled with concrete in tear ducts to stop the tears. You listen to peers of nobodies that wished for the same type of cheers, for the same type of love, caressing nature that came with the path. They listened, lied and hindered to boast out an uproaring laugh. Let the lies be spewed, let the curtain close. May the Lord have mercy on those deceitful foes. May the wrath come down and pierce their brow. Let the anointing of hell transform into the tears of those clowns. Throw the roses at my feet as I take a bow. I'll look in the stand at the watchers as they wonder, "What now?"

The supporting actress is gone. The stage play ends and the best actor is alone. Trembling on the last day on this stage, my tears fall to the ground. The varnish of the wood stains from my hurt. It's over, really over. But the haters still throw dirt. Still speak when not spoken to, still laugh about their plot. But I'm a man, a man of vengeance that knows I can make their Earth extremely hot. Bring hell to their doorstep and dismantle their dreams. Have an altar call in the midst of their ceremony and insert a deathful scream. I can shake the plates of their Earth like a Pacific earthquake. I am their ice water in the dungeon. I am their dark angel, taking their life, having them unable to wake. Run on, actress. Your role has run its duration. I'm deeply in love with you, Miss Lady. But the soul I possess can't take this new adaptation. My addiction to time has put a closed date on love. I release the birds from my heart and they symbolize black doves. I'll let them fly toward the Heaven, letting the universe speak to their pattern of flight. Disregard the past. If they come back, their feathers will be purified white.

But when will that day come? Will it happen in this lifetime at all? I can only do me, and me alone. Living someone else's life is asinine to want that on this path I roam. I am the bar! The goal of maximum achievement. I am the apex, the pinnacle. I am light years ahead thus far. I let people get close and my circle of life was destroyed. I'm tired of sitting still. Laughingly and sarcastically, I am annoyed. So the bar I sit on, I now raise it higher. To the smiling backstabbers, ignorant/feeble naysayers, I'll be your liar. I'll be the dude that's persecuted for all to see. But trust, I'll build my castle from the bricks that are thrown at me. Give y'all shovels so y'all can dig your ditches. Turn them into a moat around my fortress, add water and alligators to drown all the snitches. The gloves are off. The guns are loaded and cocked. I am never scared of my present because my future can't be stopped.

I am what you wish you were, but fine-tuned and precise. I am the exploitation of greatness. My stage play, my ultimate sacrifice. The blood of her and me shall drip as the sunset fades. Our shadows are our companions as we get lost in our days. I talk no more. I write to release my thoughts. My pen bleeds alcohol on my wounds from the battles I fought. The notepad covers the scars like bandages to hide the lacerations. Together, they are my antidote. They assist me through this permutation. I walk through life with excerpts written from my soul. I drop them along the way for the universe to hold. It embraces and listens as I speak my pain, to allow the overcast to diminish and sunshine to dry the rain. I turn my ears off, like a machine with an insufficient power supply. I gouge my old eyes out because the rain allowed them to cry. The hurt ruptured the alliance of universal souls, no parallel route or perpendicular point to hold. Enough is enough. Closure has to come from some facet or form. Understand this, reader. There are some things that are inserted into your vessel once born.

Born to die from the curse that was bitten. You're able to bless one person in life, but Heaven isn't a given. You can ask for a hand to live life with, to be one and to allow love to grow. But the ides of August can loom large and strike you down with a death blow. You can confide in the ones that need you in their world. Twist and turn your thoughts around and insert a spiral twirl. The now friends show their fiendish characteristics to replace the top spot. Pour gasoline onto warm coals, turning the Heaven I knew into a climate of hellish hot. Try to be the bigger man and forgive because of my faults. Then I bowed my head in the midst of silence and heard you bastards talk. I saw your scheme to allow my gap to spread. I wash my hands of you belligerent pessimist individuals. May the spear decapitate their heads. For my loss, may the lack of repenting bury your presence to never be re-earthed. Never can they come back around. No more catalyst diminishing our worth. I sit alone screenwriting, me along with my pen and pad. No matter what is what, I swear on everything, Miss Lady, that you are all I had. The curtains touch the wood of the stage that housed our hyphen. I love the soul of your essence. You're the inspiration to my love of writing. To the one that spoke out of turn when they weren't called upon: I thank you for weeding yourselves out. I am still royalty, holding the bar as you still have to submit. I'm done!

Demotion from Home to House

I lie in the bed that we call ours, in the house we call home. I hug the pillows to caress something you left your scent on. I walked in your room, looking for a shirt. Standing in the middle of the floor, I daydreamed of you changing your clothes in front of me for approval. Shaking my head, I walked into my room with the thoughts of listening to music. The first song was one of your favorites. I immediately sit down in the chair and pray to hear your voice sing along. So I walked to the couch that you purchased for us to lounge on. Instantly, I catch chills for the reoccurring thoughts of us lying together till we fell asleep.

I knew then that my mind was plummeting from sane to insanity. I cleaned each area of the home to have something to do, but it worsened the psyche that I call my own. I cleaned the dining room table that we sometimes ate together at. I fixed some food and sat there, looking across at an empty seat that didn't house your shell. I washed my dishes, only to reenact the times that we did them together. Times where one would just stand and talk to go over anything new that happened or of importance. I put both hands on the sink and bowed for prayer. I turned and said, "Amen!" and looked at the trash. Putting on a pair of shoes that you bought to surprise me, I smiled. I grabbed the trash and walked across the street. After turning around and staring at the house, I noticed there wasn't anyone staring at me from the windows to make sure I was going to make it back safely.

I stopped in the middle of the street and stared at the home that was stripped to house status. Walking back in, I noticed a pair of pumps you must have taken off not to get the carpet dirty. I picked them up, only to think back to the days I would rub your feet from the long days at work. I placed them on top of the shoe boxes and noticed I left the iron on. But nobody was home to yell at me. So I did it in an uproar fashion. I sat at the foot of the bed and took a deep breath, only to smell the sweet fragrances that coat your skin. I ran my hands through my hair from the pain and remembered the first time you grabbed me by my head to bring me close to your chest so I could cry from pain. This time, I cried on my own and felt my heart beating solo and not conjoined. I had to do something. So I went to the bathroom to dunce my face in water, only to raise it up and see the monster that drove you away from me.

Eyes bloodshot red from a late night of arguing and deceit on my part, I couldn't look at myself either. So I turned around to look at the wall. I closed the door to see your head scarf. I envisioned you getting ready for bed by doing your hair in the mirror. I sat on the toilet and stared out the window as I ran the hottest bath the tub could hold. I looked to the window sill and poured some of your Sweet Pea Bubble Bath into the water to give it the smell of you. I lit a Black Amethyst candle to help give me the feel of you being present. I undressed to hop into the scalding hot water and became engulfed in the aroma of the scent. Just me and the house, I listened to the noise it gave off as I laid there.

My mind started playing tricks on me. I thought I heard the door open and swore you were home. I saw lights in the driveway and prayed it was you pulling up. Letting my mind continue to race, I envisioned you getting prepared to sit in the water and allowing me to wash you down and not move a limb. None of the above was reality, so I took my head under water and wondered how long it would take to pass out. Coming to my senses, I arose to realize that I was out of character and needed to find the things that naturalized our relationship. Letting the water out of the tub, I immediately grabbed the towel and instantly smelled the fabric softener that scented the fabric. All I could see is how you slaved over the laundry to keep our clothes clean. Walking to the bedroom, I prayed I had some type of communication from you on my phone. I looked, only to find nothing. The same phone that caused us problems, the same one that housed the messages, the same one I never compromised on.

I looked thoroughly and threw it against the floor, praying it shattered. I prayed it broke, like my heart once you walked out the door. It withstood the blow, and I realized it's me. It's the lack of listening and being a doer these days. I allowed the world and the people in it to alter the man that you fell in love with. I have indulged in activities that could serve maximum lockup without a second thought. I left voids in questioning and placement, only to be implemented of a crime weeks later. I blamed you for things you had no control over. The toll of the massive damage was evident once the door closed and the conversation of no return was present. My voice cracked at the increased thought of losing the one person that I was birthed for leaving my life. We built a world and I allowed destruction to come into it, thinking we could continue to live here.

I protected you from so much over the years and, in a blink of an eye, I scared you to the point of your absence. I invaded personal property to find something that needed no clarification. I took stupidity to an all-time high and set the maker for ignorance. I allowed our world to crash and spiral out of control. I have held grudges for immeasurable times that only needed a quick conversation to fix that I wouldn't grant. I left you to fend for yourself in a time and place where it should have been us. I walk the hallways of the house that is not our home tonight. I listen for your voice to ask for something to drink or to check the heat. But I hear nothing. I yell out, "I'm sorry!" as I drop to my knees and cry for forgiveness. But the walls say nothing back. The house has been my dungeon. I have quarantined myself to answer questions. I have no one to talk to because I have driven off my support staff. So I lie in the bed we call ours, praying you call it ours again once the morning sun peaks out from the eastern horizon. I hold the pillows that nestled your body through the night and pray they give me the same comfort through this emotional night. Maybe the pillows will house the tears of my cries as I cleanse my soul to find myself.

Wondering

I messed up. I let my mind out talk my heart. I feel the soul in me fading to extinction. Life's walls have closed in on me. The life I knew feels like it was a dream. I never thought pain could reenter. But some things have their own way of forming into existence. There's nothing more heartfelt than the simultaneous beat of two hearts. There is nothing more painful than the separation of eternal love. I always said I would rather love hard than not at all. I guess I love with my head sometimes because my choices are one-sided and hard headed. My body is weak. I shake while standing. Love is my insulin and medication can't be granted. I am falling out of sanity. My mind wonders and veers down treacherous avenues. I allow them to get the best of me and end up corrupting the surrounding entities. I lost myself on this walk. I gave something up that I need back. I don't know what it is, but it is vital.

Karma is kicking my butt. It is the beat down that I wasn't looking for. I thought I had eliminated all reoccurrences for it to come back and haunt me. Obviously, I was wrong. My world is Armageddon. I don't know if there is any hope to save it. If it is, I will try my all. Whatever it needs, I will give. I pray that from my commitment, it will allow some type of vegetation for new life. I know the plains and the meadows will be scared. They will be altered from this day forward. I would rather nurse that scared land than to start fresh somewhere else. If I have to pick up the mess I dropped while walking this path, I will. Hopefully, the commitment is enough to warrant my return. I cried several nights for help. The Lord listened, but my ears had to be closed when he spoke back. I killed my future with several embellished shots to its gut. The impact may have been as severe as death.

I look to the skies to determine what I'm doing. Is love something I forgot how to do? I reminisce of days old, where carefree and no worries ran hand and hand. Now they are abundantly missing and sunny days only have overcast around me. My halo has turned to horns. There's nothing sanctified about my devilish behind. I want to be so right sometimes that my actions are extremely wrong. I prove points that later make me feel disengaged. What is the point of being right when you belittle the company you keep? Life teaches daily. Maybe my scholarly hat isn't on at all. Maybe I am coasting along, telling answers. I should be asking questions on how the problems can be solved. I have to be a solution to the equation that adds up. But if the formula is wrong, then the characters lack the right arrangement.

I was born for this person's one breath, one touch, one kiss. I felt the help that was sent from over the mountain top, but neglected to make the house a home. I know what happiness is and I've seen brighter days on the stormiest day. I saw the future and smiled at what it could be. Yet, I am alone in stance, shaking and trembling from fear of loneliness. My heart is heavy, yet I know the feeling in the universe is mutual. Nothing is more annoying than watching a sunset prematurely for the entrance of darkness. Where is there to go when the path you walk is undeveloped, when the home you stay in is a shell of nonexistence? What's the purpose of living when the life you love isn't available?

I tore it down, so I have to rebuild it. But if I needed help, would a helping hand ever come lend itself? Will that hand look me in the eye and move forward with today and tomorrow, or will the past serve as the foundation that will crumble the structure again? I guess trust is everything. Everything I got doesn't have trust in my heart. I shake my head, listen to my own nonsense, and throw all negativity out the window. I want to walk a path, holding hands, walking side by side in love. I want, but there has to be want from the second party, as well. I realized while letting my mind wonder, people change, but relationships have to grow. Where I thought I grew mine, I guess that the change needed to be addressed. Nothing was ever said and separation of hearts has occurred. I keep mine placed in the same spot, hoping that my birth partner will blanket theirs with mine. Maybe that blanket will one day allow me to fall asleep with them, our hearts and souls, in love again, heavenly loving to be in love together!

About The Author

Like a classic Picasso painting, his literary genius doesn't just leap off the pages—it gets into the heart and soul of the reader. Mirroring the style and prose of literary greats such as Robert Frost, Langston Hughes and Maya Angelou, Kefentse Booth not only paints vivid pictures with his choice of words—he immerses the reader so deep into the situation at hand that they hardly ever have time to come up for fresh air. His undeniable love for music and passion for the written (and spoken) word shape his sentences into rhythmic compositions that leave readers craving more long after they've turned the last page.

Raised by a Detroit public school educator, Booth's poetic infatuation sprouted at a very young age—landing him a poetry feature in *The Michigan Chronicle*, Detroit's oldest African-American newspaper, at the age of twelve. His obsession with the concept of love, coupled with his strong interest in community affairs and social conscious topics, led him to compile essay-style narrations, which catapulted him into writing competitions as early as high school. Supported by teachers and family, Booth soon excelled in numerous writing contests, where he greater honed his skills and learned how to engage audiences of all diversities.

Even when he attended Tuskegee University, where he obtained his Bachelor of Science in Business Administration, Booth not only played sports consistently—but he continued to pursue his exposition as he wrote about the parallels of love and life.

In his debut book, *Miles Traveled Down Love's Highway*, Booth takes readers on a journey of life lessons and the reality of relationships. No matter where readers choose to get on this sensual highway, they will experience pain, pleasure and fiery passion—even if they only read one excerpt. Written from a personal perspective of his past mishaps, mistakes and misfits, Booth strives to intertwine the realistic, yet unexpected love life of the average reader—allowing readers worldwide to not only see themselves, but *feel* themselves in the moment.

Because of his great love for all things literary, Booth founded Street Light Dreams, LLC, where he cultivates and educates writers to pursue their passion and become published authors. He resides with his wife, Fallon, in the surrounding metropolitan Detroit area.

www.ingramcontent.com/pod-product-compliance
Lightning Source LLC
Chambersburg PA
CBHW071010120726
47910CB00004B/1465